Bedtime, Little Mouse

Written by
Magali Mialaret

Illustrated by
Carmen Saldaña

A Note from the Author

Are you ready to change bedtimes forever?

Good sleep is crucial for healthy development. While sleeping, children process what they've learnt during the day, which supports brain function and emotional wellbeing. One of the greatest gifts we can give as carers is to teach them a method that will help them to fall asleep, calmly and peacefully, every night.

Follow the three-step **Mindful Bedtime Method** and help give your 'little mouse' the skills they need for a good night's sleep. It is based on years of studying how the brain works and is anchored in science and wellbeing research.

Making these steps a nightly habit will help your child develop a healthy bedtime practice. Applied regularly, it can help to improve sleep and minimize night-time anxiety.

Magali Mialaret PgC

IF YOU FEEL YOU NEED PROFESSIONAL SUPPORT OR INFORMATION ABOUT CHILDHOOD SLEEP AND ANXIETY, CONSULT YOUR FAMILY DOCTOR.

Mindful Bedtime Method

Follow these three simple steps to help your little
mouse prepare for bed and then relax into sleep.

STEP ONE

Brush teeth, wash face, put on pyjamas and make
sure your child is nice and cosy in bed. Turn the
lights down low and encourage your child to relax.

STEP TWO

Read aloud the story of *Bedtime, Little Mouse*.
Try to keep your voice, mind and body calm and
relaxed as you tell the story. Encourage your child to
do the things that Big Mouse tells Little Mouse to do
as she is helped to sleep. For example, help your child
position their cuddly toy on their chest and watch
it rise and fall at the same time as Little Mouse.

STEP THREE

If, after the story, your child is not quite ready to
drift off, turn to the back of the book and read them
practices from **More Bedtime Mindfulness**. These will
reinforce the methods introduced in the story.

Sweet dreams, little mice.

Little Mouse lives in the woods
in a cosy little mouse house.

Every morning she says hello
to the butterflies and birds ...

... and checks on the flowers,
all covered in morning dew.

As the sun shines in the sky during the day,
Little Mouse plays with her friends.

They run through the grasses that swoosh and swish, softly in the breeze.

But as the day goes by and the sun
goes down, the sky turns pink,

then orange,

then purple,
and the sunlight fades away.

Dark clouds gather and the chilly air bites.
"It's time to go home," says Little Mouse.

As the mice rush home, a storm breaks out,
and lightning flashes above.

"Quick!" say the mice, as the air shakes with thunder,
drumming, banging and booming.

They duck
under branches,

then jump over puddles,

the rain pouring down
on their heads.

They quickly scurry and scamper back home,
as the wind blows around and around.

Little Mouse rushes into Big Mouse's arms,
who dries off the droplets and makes her feel warm.
"It's time for bed, now. Quickly, hop in.
Get cosy and ready to dream."

But when Little Mouse shuts her eyes,
she can still see the flash of the storm.
The rumble of thunder whirrs in her body
and the lightning lights up her mind.

Big Mouse gives Little Mouse her favourite toy
as she snuggles down nice and warm.
"Breathe in, Little Mouse and hold your toy close.
Let it rest on your belly and watch it go up and down.

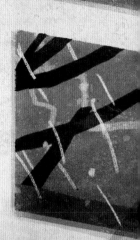

In, out, in, out,
breathe out at the end of the day."

"Use your breath to blow away the storm,
and watch your worries drift away.

A little white cloud will help them
along and chase all your fears away.

In, out, in, out, breathe out at the end of the day."

"Now that the clouds have been chased away, think of the joys of the day."

Little Mouse thinks of how happy she was when she played in the grasses that swayed.

The friendliest frogs,

the slithering snails,

the quick, swooping birds,

the colourful flowers.

"In, out, in, out, breathe out at the end of the day."

"Feel how soft your bed is. Relax your head and your toes.

Relax your neck and your whiskers.
Relax your paws and your nose.

And when you remember the joys of the day,
and the bed feels all cosy and warm, you must remember to say:

'Thank you for today.'

In, out, in, out, breathe out at the end of the day."

The sky is dark, the moon is out, magic stars shine in the sky.

In, out, in, out, and that was the end of the day.

More Bedtime Mindfulness

If your child is not ready for sleep after you have finished reading the story, encourage them to close their eyes while you read aloud one or more of the following practices. These are designed to help your little one relax, let go of the day and drift off to sleep.

Each practice has an introductory note outlining the mindful intention behind it. The actual practice, shown as: Just like Little Mouse ... should be read out loud to your child. Instructions about how to pace your reading, for example: [count to 2], will be shown in brackets. These aren't meant to be read out loud.

Practice One: Blissful Breath

Notes: This practice is designed to help your little mouse
feel calmer and more grounded in their body before sleep.

Just like Little Mouse, it's time to relax.
Hold your cuddly toy on your tummy and gently close your eyes.
Breathe in through your nose and feel your cuddly toy slowly going up.
Breathe out through your mouth and feel it coming down.

Up [count to 2] and down [count to 3].
And up [count to 2] and down [count to 3].

Notice how your toy moves up when the air comes in
and down when the air goes out.

Up [count to 2] and down [count to 3].
And up [count to 2] and down [count to 3].

Breathe out at the end of day.

Practice Two: Time to Say 'Thank You'

Notes: Before drifting off to sleep, there's one last chance to feel gratitude for all the love and kindness experienced during the day. Softly, as your child falls asleep, say 'thank you' for today.

Now, let's say thank you for all the beautiful things in your life,
little mouse. Breathe in and out very slowly, with your
cuddly toy going up and down on your tummy.

With every breath in, feel all the beauty and love,
and with every breath out say thank you.

Thank you ...
Thank you ...
Thank you ...

[Repeat two more times - feel free to add
specific things your child may feel grateful for.]

Sleep now little one, have beautiful dreams.
Tomorrow, when the sun rises,
you will have another beautiful day.

Practice Three: Marshmallow Body

Notes: Guide your little mouse through this body-scan mindfulness practice, designed for relaxation. Read it slowly, imagining that you are feeling it in your own body, too. It will help you find a gentle, slow pace in which to read the words.

Imagine you're resting on a big, fluffy marshmallow.
Keep breathing very softly and feel:

[Say these slowly, one by one.]

Your neck,
Your shoulders,
Your back,
Your left arm,
Your right arm,
Your heartbeat,
Your tummy,
Your bum,
Your legs,
Your feet and all of your toes.

All of your body is relaxed on the big,
fluffy marshmallow.

Practice Four: Special Moments

Notes: This practice helps your little mouse remember
all of the joys and precious moments of the day, so
that they can be carried forwards into tomorrow.

Breathe in and out very slowly.
Remember today's special moments:
the yummy food, the fun and games, the silly jokes,
and everything soft or shiny or tasty that you saw and felt.

With every breath, feel all the beauty and love of those memories.

Breathe in all the beauty of today, feel it
in your body and draw it into your heart.

Breathe in [count to 2] and out [count to 3].
Breathe in [count to 2] and out [count to 3].

Breathe in the joy of the day.

Practice Five: Little White Cloud

Notes: For a restful sleep, it's important to let go of
all the worries of the day. It's time for relaxed little
mice to breathe out and forget their troubles.

Imagine there's a beautiful little white cloud.
It has come to take all of your worries far, far away.
Breathe out all of your cares, now, so that the
little white cloud can carry them away.

Breathe in [count to 2] and out [count to 3].
Breathe in [count to 2] and out [count to 3].

[Repeat two more times.]

Now, take a slow, deep breath, and feel your tummy go up.
Breathe out, and blow the little white cloud away.

Breathe out at the end of day.

Author Biography

Magali Mialaret is a parent, executive coach, yoga teacher and consultant. She has spent years studying the brain, culminating in the completion of a postgraduate qualification in applied neuroscience. While raising her child, working full-time, studying yoga coaching and neuroscience, Magali realized that the work she did with grown-ups could be helpful much earlier in life.

Edited by Jonny Leighton
Designed by Jack Clucas
Cover design by John Bigwood

M.M. – Dedicating this book to my daughter, a patient editor who connected my ideas and work with a child's point of view. You are such a source of inspiration for growth.

First published in Great Britain in 2022 by Buster Books,
an imprint of Michael O'Mara Books Limited, 9 Lion Yard,
Tremadoc Road, London SW4 7NQ

W www.mombooks.com/buster f Buster Books 🐦 @BusterBooks 📷 @buster_books

Text copyright © Buster Books 2022
Illustrations copyright © Carmen Saldaña 2022
Layout and design copyright © Buster Books 2022

A CIP catalogue record for this book is available from the British Library.

ISBN: 978-1-78055-734-2

1 3 5 7 9 10 8 6 4 2

This book was printed in December 2021 by Leo Paper Products Ltd,
Heshan Astros Printing Limited, Xuantan Temple Industrial Zone,
Gulao Town, Heshan City, Guangdong Province, China.